Grandaddy's Place

Grandaddy's Place

by HELEN V. GRIFFITH

pictures by
JAMES STEVENSON

GREENWILLOW BOOKS, NEW YORK

The full-color art was
prepared as black line
with watercolor paints.
The typeface is Perpetua.

Text copyright © 1987
by Helen V. Griffith
Illustrations copyright ©
1987 by James Stevenson

Printed in Hong Kong by
South China Printing Co.
First Edition
10 9 8 7 6 5 4 3 2 1

Library of Congress
Cataloging-in-Publication Data
Griffith, Helen V.
Grandaddy's place.
Summary:
At first Janetta does not
like Grandaddy, his farm, or
his animals—but they like
her, and as she gets used to
them, she likes them too.
[1. Farm life—Fiction.
2. Grandfathers—Fiction]
I. Stevenson, James, (date)
ill. II. Title.
PZ7.G8823Gr   1987
[E]   86-19573
ISBN 0-688-06253-9
ISBN 0-688-06254-7 (lib. bdg.)

FOR JEAN BLYTHE

CHAPTER ONE

One day Momma said to Janetta, "It's time you
knew your grandaddy." Momma and Janetta went to
the railroad station and got on a train. Janetta had
never ridden on a train before. It was a long ride,
but she liked it. She liked hearing about Momma's
growing-up days as they rode along. She didn't even
mind sitting up all night.

But when they got to Grandaddy's place, Janetta didn't like it at all.

The house was old and small. The yard was mostly bare red dirt. There was a broken-down shed and a broken-down fence.

"I don't want to stay here," said Janetta.

Momma said, "This is where I grew up."

An old man came out onto the porch.

"Say hello to your grandaddy," Momma said. Janetta was too shy to say hello. "You hear me, Janetta?" Momma asked.

"Let her be," said Grandaddy.

So Momma just said, "Stay out here and play while I visit with your grandaddy."

They left Janetta standing on the porch. She
didn't know what to do. She had never been in the
country before. She thought she might sit on the
porch, but there was a mean-looking cat on the only
chair. She thought she might sit on the steps, but
there was a wasps' nest up under the roof. The
wasps looked meaner than the cat. Some chickens
were taking a dust-bath in the yard. When Janetta
came near, they made mean sounds at her.

Janetta walked away. She watched the ground for bugs and snakes. All at once a giant animal came out of the broken-down shed. It came straight toward Janetta, and it was moving fast. Janetta turned and ran. She ran past the chickens and the wasps' nest and the mean-looking cat.

She ran into the house.

"There's a giant animal out there," she said.

Grandaddy looked surprised. "First I knew of it," he said.

"It has long legs and long ears and a real long nose," said Janetta.

Momma laughed. "Sounds like the mule," she said.

"Could be," said Grandaddy. "That mule's a tall mule."

"It chased me," said Janetta.

"It won't hurt you," Momma said. "Go back outside and make friends." But Janetta wouldn't go back outside.

"Nothing out there likes me," she said.

CHAPTER TWO

After dark Momma and Grandaddy and Janetta sat out on the steps. The mean-looking cat wasn't anywhere around. Janetta hoped the wasps were asleep. She was beginning to feel sleepy herself. Then a terrible sound from the woods brought her wide awake.

"Was that the mule?" she asked.

"That was just an old hoot owl singing his song," said Grandaddy.

"It didn't sound like singing to me," said Janetta.

"If you were an owl, you'd be tapping your feet," said Grandaddy.

They sat and listened to the owl, and then Grandaddy said, "It was just this kind of night when the star fell into the yard."

"What star?" asked Janetta.

"Now, Daddy," said Momma.

"It's a fact," said Grandaddy. "It landed with a thump, and it looked all around, and it said, 'Where am I?'"

"You mean stars speak English?" asked Janetta.

"I guess they do," said Grandaddy, "because English is all I know, and I understood that star just fine."

"What did you say to the star?" asked Janetta.

Grandaddy said, "I told that star, 'You're in the United States of America,' and the star said, 'No, I mean what planet is this?' and I said, 'This is the planet Earth.'"

"Stop talking foolishness to that child," Momma said.

"What did the star say?" asked Janetta.

"The star said it didn't want to be on the planet Earth," said Grandaddy. "It said it wanted to get back up in the sky where it came from."

"So what did you do, Grandaddy?" Janetta asked.

"Nothing," said Grandaddy, "because just then the star saw my old mule."

"Was the star scared?" Janetta asked.

"Not a bit," said Grandaddy. "The star said, 'Can that mule jump?' and I said, 'Fair, for a mule,' and the star said, 'Good enough.' Then the star hopped up on the mule's back and said, 'Jump.'"

Momma said, "Now, you just stop that talk."

"Don't stop, Grandaddy," said Janetta.

"Well," Grandaddy said, "the mule jumped, and when they were high enough up the star hopped off and the mule came back down again."

"Was the mule all right?" asked Janetta.

"It was thoughtful for a few days, that's all," said Grandaddy.

Janetta stared up at the sky. "Which star was it, Grandaddy?" she asked.

"Now, Janetta," Momma said, "you know that's a made-up story."

Grandaddy looked up at the stars. "I used to know," he said, "but I'm not sure anymore."

"I bet the mule remembers," Janetta said.

"It very likely does," said Grandaddy.

From somewhere in the bushes some cats began to yowl. "That's just the worst sound I know," Momma said. "Janetta, chase those cats."

"They're just singing their songs," said Grandaddy.

"That's right, Momma," said Janetta. "If you were a cat, you'd be tapping your feet."

Momma laughed and shook her head. "One of you is as bad as the other," she said.

CHAPTER THREE

The next day Grandaddy and Janetta went fishing. Janetta had never been fishing before. She didn't like it when Grandaddy put a worm on the hook.

"Doesn't that hurt him?" she asked.

"I'll ask him," said Grandaddy. He held the worm up in front of his face. "Worm, how do you feel about this hook?" he asked. He held the worm up to his ear and listened. Then he said to Janetta, "It's all right. That worm says there's nothing he'd rather do than fish."

"I want to hear him say that," Janetta said. She took the worm and held it up to her ear. "He's not saying anything," she said.

"That worm is shy," said Grandaddy. "But I know he just can't wait to go fishing." Grandaddy threw the line into the water. It wasn't long before he caught a fish. Then he gave Janetta the pole so that she could try. She threw the line in, and before long she had a fish, too. It was just a little fish. Janetta looked at it lying on the bank. It was moving its fins and opening and closing its mouth.

"I think it's trying to talk," Janetta said.

"It may be, at that," said Grandaddy. He held the fish up to his ear. "It says, 'Cook me with plenty of cornmeal,'" said Grandaddy.

"I want to hear it say that," said Janetta.

"Can you understand fish-talk?" asked Grandaddy.

"I don't know," said Janetta.

"Well, all that fish can talk is fish-talk," said Grandaddy.

Janetta held the fish up to her ear and listened. "It says, 'Throw me back,'" Janetta said.

Grandaddy looked surprised. "Is that a fact?" he asked.

"Clear as anything," said Janetta.

"Well, then I guess you'd better throw it back," said Grandaddy.

Janetta dropped the little fish into the water and watched it swim away. Grandaddy threw the line back in and began to fish again. "I never saw anybody learn fish-talk so fast," he said.

"I'm going to learn worm-talk next," said Janetta.

CHAPTER FOUR

When they had enough fish for supper, Janetta and Grandaddy walked on home. The mean-looking cat came running to meet them. He purred loud purrs and rubbed against their legs.

"I didn't know that cat was friendly," Janetta said.

"He's friendly when you've been fishing," said Grandaddy.

The mule came out of the shed and walked toward them with its ears straight up. Janetta didn't know whether to run or not. The mule walked up to her and pushed her with its nose. Janetta was sorry she hadn't run.

"What do you know," Grandaddy said. "That old mule likes you."

"How can you tell?" Janetta asked.

"It only pushes you that way if it likes you," said Grandaddy.

"Really?" asked Janetta.

"It's a fact," said Grandaddy. "Up until now that mule has only pushed me and the cat and one of the chickens." Janetta was glad she hadn't run. She reached out her hand and touched the mule's nose.

"Grandaddy," she said, "What's the mule's name?"

"Never needed one," said Grandaddy. "It's the only mule around."

"Can I name it?" asked Janetta.

"You surely can," said Grandaddy.

Janetta thought. "I could call it Nosey," she said.

"That would suit that mule fine," said Grandaddy.

Janetta thought some more. "Maybe I'll call it Beauty," she said.

"That's a name I never would have thought of," said Grandaddy.

The mule gave Janetta another push. "This mule really likes me," Janetta said. "It must know I'm going to give it a name."

"You don't have to give it anything," said Grandaddy. "That mule just likes you for your own self."

CHAPTER FIVE

After supper Grandaddy and Momma and Janetta sat out on the steps and watched the night come on. The stars began to show themselves, one by one.

"Now I know what I'll name that mule," Janetta said. "I'll call it Star."

"Should have thought of that myself," said Grandaddy.

"Tomorrow I'll give the cat a name," said Janetta.

"Only fair, now the mule has one," said Grandaddy.

"After I get to know the chickens, I'll name them, too," said Janetta. "Then you'll be able to call them when you want them."

"That'll be handy," said Grandaddy.

"You'll be naming the hoot owl next," Momma said.

"I've been thinking about it," said Janetta.

Momma laughed, and Grandaddy did, too.
"Now, how did we get along around here
before you came?" he asked.
"I've been wondering that, too, Grandaddy,"
said Janetta.